THE
FUTURE HISTORY
OF
HUMANITY

PART ONE

LOGAN UBER

Published by Polydimensional Publishing an imprint of The Brothers Uber, Grove City, PA.

The Brothers Uber
www.brothersuber.com

First Edition • Text Edition 1.0 (Print Edition)

ISBN: 978-1-943933-03-7

Printed in the United States of America

FOR C.U.

This is not a light book, the content herein is meant to challenge you, the reader. The subjects undertaken and presented are at times shocking and potentially unnerving. At the same time, this book is meant to be one heavy on theme and light on details, many items are left up to the imaginings of you, the reader. The journey of this book transcends the contemporary and steps into the future, a future not so far distant from our own, and though the characters and companies may seem to share similarities with entities today, those similarities are purely coincidental and not purposefully done. I hope that you enjoy this first installment into the future and are able to look past any shortcomings that I, the recorder of said events, might have.

Logan Uber

Part One

1

"Eggs. Eggs fresh from my daughter's womb" came the call of the door-to-door salesman, his briefcase heavy with the wares of life. In reality they weren't even real eggs, more chemical fabrication than any real genetic offspring. He was considered old-fashioned in his door-to-door approach, most companies had long since outsourced physical interactions with clients to the virtual world. He preferred the personal touch, said it helped to seal the deal with a physical handshake. Without some type of physical touch in the process, manufacturing life just seemed wrong, like an abomination.

Sales had been slow as of late, with the widespread adoption of CRISPR/Cas9 editing and the recent breakthrough in the mass market manufacture of the CRISPR components genetic manipulation and editing was no longer reserved for the super-wealthy. The sudden availability of cheap genetic editing had crashed the luxury designer market overnight. It was going to take more than a few fancy advertisements to convince people to mortgage their child's future on a few extra genes.

Initially, genetic manipulation was considered taboo, like tampering with God's handiwork would bring on the apocalypse. Even today there still exist pockets of resistance, radical free-birth movements and groups vehemently opposed to the idea of improving the human condition. In the early days, opposition was fierce, even deadly. Many on the forefront were assassinated by those fearful of the future. It took years to get approval to work on removing negative hereditary genes, those responsible for congenital disorders, chronic diseases like hemophilia, and inherited vulnerabilities to cancer. Once it became a matter of compassion restrictions quickly relaxed, greased by the flow of money.

Flawless skin, the right eye and skin color, the perfect dimpled smile became the new rage for the super-wealthy. Strength, endurance, and intellect became the rallying cry for the super-desperate. As people became more and more desperate they turned to darker forms of financing. Seeking to capitalize on the need for capital investors quickly lobbied governments for approval of a new financial marketplace. Would-be leaders quickly took up the cause, sensing the rapid shift in societal views. The pink market emerged on a quiet spring day with little fanfare to announce the advent of change. Within weeks it had grown to rival the smaller financial exchanges.

Even then there were calls to slow down, to take a step back and not rush headlong into an unknown future. There were early failures; childhood injuries that ended future mega-athlete careers before they could even begin to think about taking flight. Musicians who lost the will to play before they became the childhood prodigies they were designed to be. Performance clauses quickly became the rule of the day and insurance against such failures the hottest new item. It became relatively simple for the would-be parents of future stars to mortgage their child's future for the simple pleasures of the day. Why struggle and work when you can just sell shares against your child's future performance? If you invested wisely, picked the right gene combinations, you could make millions now and reap the benefits forever.

Picking the right combination, balancing costs against possible future performance required more than a simple brochure or advertisement. It required a personal touch, a door-to-door salesman who would sit down with you, look you right in the eye and guarantee that God himself couldn't make a more perfect child. You didn't get to be salesman of the year by sitting behind a virtual terminal interacting with fake avatars. And so, he walked with his clarion call of "Eggs. Eggs fresh from my daughter's womb" down that old dusty street.

2

She ruled them, not in a kind benevolent leader type of way, but more as a slave master waiting to extract perfection from the blood and toil of those beneath her. She didn't fear them; they were conditioned from birth to serve their would-be masters and benefactors. Their very existence was the result of health fund managers like her, pooling the wealthy and the financially savvy to invest in an unknown future based upon returns precipitated on genetic manipulation. She was a visionary in her field and built her company from a small theoretical think tank into globe spanning conglomeration. The sun never set, because there was no end to her company. As she liked to say, the sun was always rising and with it her company.

While others had invested in better and better entertainers, musicians, athletes, actors and actresses she invested in knowledge. When others invested in technology scientists, researchers, innovators and inventors she invested in biology. It was her company and her team that had broken the barrier for the mass manufacture of CRISPER

"

components. She drove her company hard and her team harder. She wasn't satisfied with CRISPER/Cas9; she wanted more, she wanted real time manipulation of the genome, post-birth. True, CRISPER/Cas9 allowed for limited manipulation post-birth, but its effectiveness tended to be limited to areas of breakdown due to age and/or disease. It could repair the broken parts, but it couldn't create unlimited access to the complete genetic code.

Early days of the CRISPER10 research program focused on more advanced bacterial carriers, but in the end they failed due to their tendency to breakdown over time. There were even the dark days when viral carriers were used, which too often proved fatal and uncontrollable. Many research labs were forcibly evacuated and sealed off to prevent the spread of contagions. A few were quarantined with the workers inside, becoming mass graves for both the workers and the subjects. She considered them all a few minor setbacks. The lives of her workers were numbers in a spreadsheet; she had long since purchased their souls from the compassionate parents wanting a better life for their progeny.

The parents thought it was a blessing when one of her representatives would come calling. They brought tales of immediate wealth, of the perfect baby, and of a guaranteed job for their would-be child. The benefits outweighed concerns about working conditions. Who really cared about how much their children would get paid, how long they would work, and where they would work? Immediate gratification quickly overcame and guided their judgments. Nobody cared about the darker side of the pink market, of forced servitude and labor to pay off a debt never bargained for. Pay became meaningless as wages were garnished for debt payments, dividend payouts, and contracts were executed.

The pre-birth market was the hardest to time, you never quite knew which way a child would develop. Middle market was more understandable, usually the child's personality began to shine through and their aptitude for future endeavors manifested possible returns. The real prodigies could still be invested in with room for growth, but often times by the time they were discovered their futures were secured at rates outside of the normal investor's reach. The late market was shaped by pubescent mood swings and uncontrollable rebellion against authority. For those not already prodigies this is when their value would normally crash, never to fully recover. For those without insurance against loss of value, they would become regulated to working whatever job they could find to pay off the initial investments plus guaranteed interest and a pro-rated expected rate of return. There were a few late bloomers, but the senior market saw little to no growth beyond the values established by the late market.

She'd invested heavily in the pre-birth market when it was just starting out. Quickly selling her positions in prodigies meant for entertainment and technology. With those proceeds she was able to offset her losses from disappointments. Her whole employee base owed her in one way or another and when workers are free expansion is easy. The CRISPER component-manufacturing breakthrough had made her an overnight success and allowed her to take on more ambitious projects. And so she found herself overseeing the development of CRISPER11, a new evolution in genetic manipulation.

3

You didn't become the top researcher for a global corporation by being a slacker. At least that's what he told himself every morning when he woke up. In truth it was as much a matter of genetic destiny as it was a matter of perseverance. He'd been purchased before he was even conceived, bought for a paltry sum, a gamble based on genetic potential. As an investment he had paid off immensely, even on the senior market shares of him continued to grow. The company had made back their investment by the time he was in the late market and still they extracted every little bit they could get from him. Between the pressure of burdensome performance clauses, adjusted and increasing projected rates of return, and guaranteed interest that had been deferred and then capitalized he was forced to take advantage of the company housing and food. Those in turn were added to the theoretical debt of his worth as an investment, a debt he had no part in undertaking.

Each day he woke he had to remind himself of his position and the need to not slack. He was a savant in the field of biomechanical engineering, merging the realms of nanotechnology, biology, chemistry, and energy based physics. His designs revolutionized prosthetics. This in turn added value to the company's bottom line, which in turn adjusted upwards his expected rate of return, which in turn added to his debt to the company. His upward trajectory was in reality a downward spiral of servitude.

Today was going to be different. He had cracked the code. All this time they had been focusing on the wrong components. The issue with CRISPER11 research was the natural breakdown of any nanotechnology over time. Utilizing various alloys and regulating exposure time for the nano-bots failed to prevent long-term wear and its associate breakdown. True, such techniques were able to extend the lifecycle and through theoretical models the associated life expectancy could be measured in centuries, but that wasn't the issue, that wasn't his mandate. His job was to create a single system that would allow for real time genetic manipulation in the subject indefinitely.

The breakthrough occurred when he was musing over the ingredients in the new supplements the company doctor had prescribed based on his latest lab results. There were enough minerals and chemicals within the body for a self-replicating nanite to harvest and use to make nanites and nano-bots. As long as the subject continued eating a balanced diet they would be able to fuel the objects of eternity. It would require careful analysis to determine the correct rate of reproduction so as to not overwhelm the subject's body with nanites and nano-bots while still maintaining levels sufficient to carry out the requisite real time genetic manipulation. Utilizing a hybrid of organics and nanotech the necessary minerals and chemicals could be extracted via the organics without causing stress to the subject, while the nanotech manufactured the new nanites and nano-bots. Such a synthesis would require an immense amount of finesse and tax the limits of his understanding of biomechanical engineering. But today he was going to do it.

4

She huddled quietly in the shadows of her cell. Legs bent in front of her, arms wrapped around them holding them and stopping them from shaking as she gently rocked herself back and forth. She was young, not quite ten if you trusted her physical appearance. Day after day it was the same thing, men in masks and suits, faces covered with one way see through helmets; with their needles and scalpels, cutting, slicing, extracting. It was all she could remember, all she knew.

No one ever spoke directly to her. They just grabbed and pulled, pushed and shoved. The pain was unending, the cutting her only relief. She never slept. Hers was the nightmare of the damned.

The hushed tones, the fear in their voices mixed with admiration and horror, let her know that she was an abomination. Questions of how she was still alive let her know that she shouldn't exist. Talk of CRISPER10, the project, and what happened last time let her know that she meant nothing to them. She was an object for study and experimentation. She couldn't even remember her name, if she ever had one, of that she doubted. She was supposed to be dead, of that she was certain.

She welcomed death, she longed for it, but it never came. And so she rocked herself in the corner of her cell waiting for the cutting to begin again.

Time had no meaning here and even more so for her, because she never aged.

5

The old dusty street led to a secluded cul-de-sac with a single walled estate. Not to be put off by the impressive façade the door-to-door salesman strode confidently up the walkway leading to the estate. The gate was unlatched and so the salesman let himself in. Up the long drive he marched taking in the splendor of the grounds, the tall trees, the well-groomed lawns, the flowering gardens, and carefully sculpted landscaping.

The front door was a large ominous behemoth of solid wood set in a perfectly shaped recess within the estate's marble face. The clouded veins of the marble seemed to move and shift in the light of the setting sun. There was no electronic call box, no discernable means of virtual communication. A single large iron ring hung upon the door, positioned just below eye level. The grain of the wooden door seemed to part around the ring, as if the tree had grown around it. Not to be dissuaded by the abject declaration of a rejection of technology, the salesman lifted the ring and let it fall once. Its impact carried with it no accompanying sound, as if the very act emanated silence.

The would-be salesman waited. And waited. Time seemed to freeze in that moment between sunset and dusk. The vibrant hues of the fiery setting sun splashed across the marble while shadows began to dance across the lawns. There were no sounds, only silence. In the eerie silence of the moment the would-be salesman became unnerved. He noticed the lack of sound, the deafening silence of reality, which should have been interrupted by the chorus of nature. There should have been something, a rustle of the wind, the call of a bird, the random bark of a dog, but there was nothing.

Without fanfare or noise the door began to open slowly, inwardly. The warmth of the house, a sharp contrast to the sudden drop in ambient temperature, beckoned to the would-be salesman. The interior passageway was lit with a soft glow that seemed to just exist, no source visible or detectable. As he crossed the threshold the smell of citrus assaulted his nose and the tickle of tangerines danced upon his palate. As if his other senses had been heightened by the silence of the outside world. Slowly the would-be salesman walked the length of the hallway until he came to an intersecting corridor. To the left was an atrium filled with exotic plants, while to the right was a set of double doors.

There were no sounds within the estate, no creak to the floors, no footsteps to be heard, no whispers to deceive. No people to encounter.

The would-be salesman turned right and approached the doors. As he raised his fist to knock the doors slowly opened. The doors opened upon a spiral staircase leading downward. A quiet voice is the back of his mind called out, telling him to flee, to run away and never comeback. The would-be salesman ignored the voice and descended into the depths of the estate.

6

He heard her silent tears as he sat in his cell. He felt her pain. He crouched in the middle of his cell as if the focal point on some grand stage. The guards and scientists rarely visited him. Their trips becoming less and less frequent as the years had progressed. He welcomed their visits, for with each visit came new strength. He was the nameless one, the one that woke them in the middle of the night, cold sweat pouring over their bodies, afraid of the dark and the light. Many had come, many had visited, but few remained. He would outlive and outlast all of them, an undying abomination.

7

His entry into the lab was quick and forceful. He had no time to waste if he was to succeed by sundown. His research team barely acknowledged his presence, fearing eye contact would result in them being assigned even more work. They were not as gifted as he was, not a matter of conceit, but rather a matter of fact.

He knew whom he could trust and who would be the most useful to his cause. Without missing a beat he called out their names as he strode past, summoning them to his office. As he entered his office, which was more of a conference room, the others were already filing in quietly after him. They had long since learned the penalty for delay.

He addressed them quickly, without consulting notes, for he knew exactly what had to be done. No notes were taken, and none were allowed, you didn't become part of the special projects team with the aid of notes. His directions were simple and direct, there would be no tolerance for failure, any tasks not completed in time will result in immediate termination from the program and dismissal from the company. His standards were impossibly high, but he would accept nothing less.

At sundown he was to have a meeting with her, and one did not attend a meeting with the head of the company empty handed. He would offer her a solution to the problem at hand or his resignation. There would be success or failure, he was unable to continue the drudgery of his mundane work with the ever-mounting pressure and need to succeed to satisfy his shareholders.

8

The would-be salesman descended the stone staircase, his footsteps echoing silence in the confined space. As he drew closer to the depths of the estate the air grew warmer and warmer. After what seemed like an eternity he reached the base of the staircase that opened to a long hallway with a single door at its end. The door was old and scarred with the mysteries of time. It was cracked and broken, fused together with slats of iron. There was no handle and it gave no indication that it had moved in years.

The would-be salesman approached the door, sure of his purpose as the scent of citrus grew stronger.

As he approached the door it cracked and split, shattering into a thousand pieces as the iron slats holding it together turned to dust. The room beyond consisted of a single desk, simple in design with no embellishments to speak of. Seated behind the desk in a high backed wooden chair was an impeccably dressed older gentleman, with a three-piece suit of black, a white shirt, and a blood red tie.

The man spoke, his voice raspy with age, "I've been calling for you for years, why have you not answered?"

"The time of your redemption is not of your choosing," was the salesman's curt reply.

"I beg of you, let it end," pleaded the man, his eyes misting with pain.

"It will not end so easily, your time is not yet up. There is still work for you to do," replied the salesman, showing no compassion towards the old man's pain.

"What shall I do?" begged the old man.

"There is one who must be set free and one to be rescued. One with no name and one with lost innocence," spoke the salesman as if repeating a memorized script.

"Who are they and how will I know them?" pleaded the old man.

"You know who they are and what you must do," answered the salesman cutting the old man's questions short.

After a moment's pause, the old man's eyes widened in fear. He licked his suddenly dry and parched lips, trying to gather courage from their cracked and scarred surfaces. "Must I?" was all that he managed to utter before his voice cracked in fear.

"You must. And only then will your debt be paid sufficiently for redemption" replied the salesman as he turned to leave.

Calling out, his voice hollow with the stress of too many years, the old man asked, "Will it be quickly?"

His only answer was the silence of the departure of the salesman.

9

The first breakthrough happened shortly before noon.

By one o'clock the research team was working furiously to fully integrate the biological and mechanical components into a single unified component.

Four o'clock found the team working feverishly trying to beat the daunting and unforgiving deadline.

The next three hours were steeped in models and simulations attempting to find the right balance of replication rate versus the natural breakdown cycle.

Success came after twelve grueling hours of work and with that information the top researcher headed for his seven-thirty appointment with the head of the company.

10

The researcher arrived shortly before the appointed time, and so he waited patiently and quietly outside the door. She has a strict rule that meetings began precisely on time and ended exactly at their scheduled close. "Precision isn't just for watchmakers" was her go to phrase when chiding anyone who attempted to vary from the appointed schedule.

As he waited quietly in the foyer on the top floor of the company's headquarters he allowed himself a moment to relax to appreciate the view. The foyer was flanked by two rows of windows, one row overlooking the city and the other peering out towards the horizon where the ocean meets the sky. The tiled floor of the foyer was black with luminescent speckles. Coupled with the clear ceiling it evoked a sense of weightlessness for those finding themselves in the foyer on a clear night, seemingly surrounded by stars above and stars below. The woodwork of the doors was carefully inlaid into a mural of history etched and carved into the dark hardwood wall opposite the elevators. The elevators themselves were recessed into a plain wood lined wall. The juxtaposition of the plainness of the elevator wall with the starkness of the tiled floor and the magnificence of the far wall made it abundantly clear that one was not meeting with any mere mortal.

At precisely seven-thirty he knocked once and then stepped back from the double doors. Slowly the doors opened as if of their own volition and he entered in. His strides were purposeful and without hesitation as he marched smartly into the center of the room, refusing to blink and shield his eyes from the bright setting sun. She sat behind her desk in a simple chair, framed by the setting sun, a silhouette of power.

He stood there quietly, waiting for her to speak first. The seconds ticked by, the length of their moments seeming to stretch on into eternity. After what seemed like an unbearable amount of time she broke the silence.

"I've always admired that about you, your ability to maintain your composure and your place in spite of the situation at hand."

"Thank you," was his only reply.

"What news do you bring me today?"

"The CRISPER11 project is now complete. We've created a hybrid bio-mechanical nanite that will utilize the minerals and resources from the subject's body to create more nanites and nano-bots that can then facilitate the real time genetic manipulation of the host indefinitely. The nanites can be calibrated to match the subject's physical properties to always maintain a sufficient level of nanites and nano-bots to maintain that ability as long as the subject continues to consume a balanced diet," he stated matter-of-factly.

"When will it be ready for implementation?"

At her question he withdrew a vial of luminescent blue liquid from his pocket and set it gently upon her desk. "This is the first batch and ready for injection. The nanites will automatically adjust their production parameters to match the subject's requirements. Future batches will not include that ability, requiring would-be clients to maintain a regimen of treatment with the company until those thresholds are reached, allowing for the maximization of revenues from each new client," he elaborated.

"Very well. You may now leave," she answered curtly.

Her tone made it apparent that he was dismissed. Slightly shocked and a little confused he quickly turned and headed for the exit; there was still fifteen minutes scheduled for the meeting. He hadn't even reached the doors and she was already picking up the vial and calling for a personal transport. The only thought he had as he rode the elevator down was that something big was happening and he was the cause of it.

11

Visitors rarely came in the dark of the night. She knew it was night because of the quiet, the silence of the cellblock. The quiet amplified the solitude of her existence and accentuated the companionship of her pain. As she crouched in the corner, slowly rocking herself in time with the beating of her heart, she became alerted to a commotion at the end of the hallway.

She heard voices speaking rapidly and as a single set of footsteps drew near she heard one voice rise above the rest, "you can't see her without protective gear on."

Suddenly the footsteps stopped and silence reverberated through the cellblock as if the world had suddenly gone deaf. A woman's voice, somehow familiar, spoke calmly and forcefully, the quiet stillness of her voice conveying a sense of power to reinforce her words, "Your resignation is accepted and your failure is noted."

Immediately the footsteps began again bearing the woman closer and closer. As the woman rounded the corner she immediately crouched down and placed her right hand

28

on the glass partition separating the cell from the hallway. In her left hand she held a vial of blue liquid that glowed in the dimness of the corridor. Quietly, her voice trembling slightly, the woman called out "Sister, I love you."

Workers appeared in the doorway wearing their full body protective suits that hid their genders and their identities. The woman handed the vial to the lead worker who quickly prepared it for injection. And then they came, the door opened and the workers rushed into the cell, grabbing her and holding her in place. Two workers held her legs, as two more held her arms, while they fifth worker rapidly injected the blue liquid into her left thigh, causing an immediate cascade of pain that left her convulsing on the floor as the workers retreated from their work.

After thirty seconds of mind-numbing pain and spasms, which seemed to stretch on into eternity, she curled herself into a ball in the middle of the cell and laid there, too weak to drag her broken body back to her corner.

The woman continued to look on from her crouched position, observing the rise and fall of her sister's side as she breathed in each labored breath. Her voice was quiet, lost without its normal power, "Sister, I've done it. I've found the cure to your pain. I'm sorry it's taken so long. I'm sorry I've made you wait so long."

After an eternity of silence measured in minutes, the woman spoke once more, her voice cracking with emotion, "Sister, do you even remember me?"

The seconds ticked on, with no response, and no movement, save the steady rise and fall of the girl's chest, lying broken in the middle of the cell.

"I should have visited sooner, but I couldn't bear to see you in pain. I did it all for you, and I'd do it all over again. Please forgive me and know that I love you. We'll have a lot of catching up to do once you're fully cured." the woman whispered through the glass partition.

After another ten minutes of silence the woman rose and departed with significantly less commotion than her arrival. After the woman left, the girl drug herself slowly across the smooth cold floor of the cell to rest once more in her favorite corner, slowly rocking herself in time to the beating of her heart.

12

The old man's vehicle came to a halt in front of a nondescript warehouse in a nondescript part of the city. The endless rows of warehouses created a landscape of monotony, of a bland blight of storage. He waited patiently for the twenty seconds it took his attendant to exit the front passenger seat and open his door. The impact of the base of his cane on the sidewalk echoed in the near stillness of the warehouse district. Each step, each beat brought a new crisp clap to the otherwise silent area.

His slow, deliberate pace followed a beeline path to the side doorway of one of the warehouses. When he was three paces away from the door it was flung open and a slightly panting guard, his suit barely able to contain the girth of his muscles, quickly apologized, stating "director, we did not expect you this late at night."

"Time is irrelevant" was the old man's reply as he quickly slipped through the doorway.

Once inside, the old man's path took him through a maze of crates and equipment to a far corner of the warehouse. A seemingly, unassuming doorway was opened at his approach. The room inside was a small alcove, of the type that would be used to store janitorial supplies. After a slight delay, once the door was closed the room began to descend. Once the room had fully descended the door was opened to reveal a long sterile hallway flanked with glass windows looking into laboratories filled with experiments in various stages of completion.

The old man's journey took him past the laboratories and to a heavily secured doorway at the terminal end of the hallway. The door was a large metal behemoth that stood out in stark contract to the pristine whiteness of the rest of the area. As the old man approached the doorway, two guards quickly appeared, blocking his path, as if they had materialized out of thin air. The more imposing guard spoke, simply stating "you cannot enter at this time."

"There are no restrictions for one such as I" was the old man's reply, neither stopping or altering his pace.

The guard faltered at the quiet forcefulness of the old man's statement and in the moment the old man continued his journey down the hallway to stop directly in front of the guard.

With trepidation in his voice the guard merely stated "I cannot let you pass."

"Very well, you are relieved of your duty with the company" was the old man's quiet reply.

The guard's eyes widened at the old man's words and further still as he cocked his head to one side as if trying to better hear a communication being relayed via an earpiece. He immediately stepped aside, offered his apology, and looking at the other guard simply said "I am relieved of my duties." With that he walked down the hallway to the closet elevator and left.

The remaining guard quickly opened the door and allowed the old man to pass. Beyond the doorway was a spiraling staircase cut directly into the bedrock of the area leading further into the depths of the earth. The base of the stairs opened into another long hallway, this one flanked by observation cells, some occupied, many empty. At the far end of the hallway it opened into a large laboratory with various suits hanging on the far walls. In the center of the far wall was an airlock like opening sealing off the lab from another area. The old man quickly traversed the hallway and the laboratory. Ignoring the many suits her proceeded through the airlock and down another long corridor.

His path eventually stopped before the cell of the nameless one. He rested his weary body upon the support of his cane and waited. Time seemed to stretch on forever;

seconds lengthened and merged into minutes. The minutes grew and time seemed to stand still. After a segment of eternity had passed the nameless one spoke quietly asking "have you come to finish what you started?"

"Alas, I cannot" was the old man's reply.

"Then you have cursed me and your damnation will be eternal" the nameless one spoke, unbridled fury coloring his every word.

"My path is no longer mine" the old man responded.

"Then we are both doomed."

"Not true, your path is just beginning" the old man retorted. "Your freedom with come with a price, a burden even I cannot fathom," continued the old man, "and your salvation shall seal my fate."

"What would I do?" questioned the nameless one.

"There is one whose destiny is not yet decided, you must save her, serve her, and protect her until her time has come" answered the old man.

"Who?"

"You know the one"

"When does my journey begin?"

"Now" responded the old man as he slammed his cane three times upon the floor. With the third strike the base of the cane began to glow a soft orange. As the old man rolled the cane across the floor to the cell, the glow grew in intensity, becoming a fiery red and then blinding white. As the brightness grew in intensity a small pop sounded followed by a shockwave that reverberated down the corridor knocking the few researchers in the hallway over.

13

As he rose to his full height, his joints cracking into place and echoing down the corridor, the nameless one's presence seemed to grow to fill the now open cell. His steps into the corridor projected power. The few researchers still in the area fled quickly, as mice scurrying before a feral cat.

The nameless one ignored the old man, who had managed to stay upright in spite of the shockwave, and stalked his way down the corridor. One brave and foolish guard rushed to stop and progress and was immediately tossed aside to lay unconscious at the base of the wall. In a matter of moments the nameless one found the cell that he was looking for.

14

She sensed his presence as he approached. She did not fear him, but felt no inclination to move towards him. As the nameless one stopped before her cell her rocking stopped, but otherwise there was no outward indication of her recognizing his presence.

"It is time" was all he said, his voice laced with trepidation and uncertainty.

The silence of her response seemed to form an impenetrable barrier.

The nameless one's voice echoed the hollowness of the unsure as he asked her "would you come with me?"

"I will" was her only response, her words conveying one answer, while her unmoving body another.

The nameless one dragged the unconscious guard across the hallway and used his palm print to open her cell. As the door opened she weakly lifted up her arms, as a child wishing to be carried. Without a moment's hesitation the nameless one crossed the expanse of the cell, scooped her up and hurried back into the hallway.

The journey to the airlock was fast. As the inner seal leading to laboratory opened up the nameless one rushed through the still opening door, cradling the girl in his arms and shielding her with his body from the spray of crowd control elements. The tear gas stung his eyes, the rubber bullets bruised his body, and the beanbags echoed the sounds of flesh.

His movements were fast, a blur in the chaos of the moment. The guards fell quickly, one after another, unable to stop his brutal onslaught. The rage he had kept locked up inside of him all of the years he had spent in the cell unleashed upon the world. Within moments they were making their way up the spiral staircase keeping pace to the crescendo of the blaring alarms.

The secure door at the top of the staircase, all but impenetrable to the outside world, opened easily from the inside. The single guard greeted them with a hail of bullets that ricocheted off the door and the walls. One ripped through the flesh of the nameless one's shoulder to lodge within the wall.

With a howl the nameless one lunged forward biting the guard's arm and tearing his flesh. The guard dropped his gun in response to the pain and the trauma of his injury. His body followed his gun to the floor knocked down by the nameless one's continued onslaught. Withering under the relentless fury of the nameless one's kicks the guard curled into a fetal position that began as a strong cocoon, but slowly loosened as he began to lose his grip on reality and consciousness, succumbing to the nameless one's blows.

On the edge of darkness, sure that he would never see the light of another day, he heard the faint voice of a child cry out "Stop! He doesn't deserve this. I cannot stand his pain."

As rapidly as the kicking had begun, it suddenly stopped. With a final push of the leg the guard was slid to the side of the hallway, left to lay in an ever growing pool of his blood.

The journey up the elevator shaft was accomplished without too much difficulty, as the nameless one pulled them up with his uninjured arm, while he cradled the girl with his rapidly healing injured arm. By the time they had reached the warehouse level his shoulder was completely healed, only a trail of sticky blood gave any indication of a past injury. The maze of crates and equipment did little to slow the fugitives progress, as did the guard who stayed as a sentinel at the exit.

As they exited the warehouse, the old man's attendant opened the door to the old man's car. "He said you'd be coming and that I was to take you to the edge of the city" was his only words.

As the nameless one went to turn his back to the attendant, the girl spoke, her words soft with a timeless tiredness "trust him."

The nameless one recanted his movements and quickly entered the vehicle, his muscles tense and ready in case the vehicle turned out to be a mobile prison. The ride was quick, the director's vehicle was afforded access to the expressway reserved for the rich and powerful, and before long they found themselves deposited at the outskirts of the city. Without hesitation the driver turned his vehicle back to the city and sped away into the night leaving them alone under the stars.

15

As the commotion died down following the departure of the girl and the nameless one the salesman made his way quietly through the crowds of response personnel, winding his way through the throngs of workers to a quiet corner of the cellblock. There sitting quietly upon a three legged wooden stool sat the old man. Looking up at the quiet approach of the salesman his only words were "it is done."

Without missing a beat, the salesman's reply, echoing a quiet power, was simply "it is time."

The old man reached out his hands, worn and leathery with the passing of time, grasping the outstretched hand of the salesman. As their hands clasped together a visible peace passed over the old man's face and he slumped back supporting his body on the angled meetings of the corridor's corner. His eyes closed and he released a final breath no longer burdened by the cares of life.

The salesman departed as quietly as he had come. No one moved to prevent his departure and an outside observer would have noted that no one gave any indication that he was even there.

16

Tucked away within the news of the morning was a single reference to an issue at one of the company's research centers. The company's top researcher stared seemingly into the depths of space as he contemplated what he had just read for the fifth time. Upon hearing the news, but not really hearing it he had immediately called up the transcript of the report. After going over and contemplating all possibilities he summoned his virtual assistant and immediately demanded a full accounting of what had occurred.

The reports while numerous in nature failed to illuminate what had occurred. Internal security reports provided little information beyond what the public reports had already provided. As he dug deeper into the issue at hand he encountered layers and layers of security protocols that quickly gave way to his brutal assault on the vulnerabilities of the system. He read faster and faster, viewing footage at speeds beyond the ability of a normal human to comprehend. His genetic superiority allowing him access to additional processing power and soon he was viewing the internal footage of the prior night in excess of twenty feeds simultaneously.

His eyes widened as realization registered, of the truth of what he had done by driving his team to success the day before. His search expanded into the depths of the company's secrets and as his disgust grew, so too did his fear. Time blurred, its passage masked by the drama of discovery.

His barreling train of thought, discovery, and investigation came to an immediate and unceremonious halt, disturbed by the alarm from the company's notification system alerting him to an adjustment to his expected rate of return. His value to the company had more than doubled overnight as a result of yesterday's discovery. The company had quickly recognized the power of his team's contribution and what it would mean for next year's bottom line. The juxtaposition of the atrocity that he had unknowingly helped to create and the value that the company placed on such actions destroyed the last shreds of dedication that he had to the company.

He quickly gathered all the evidence he could, compiling it on a number of data disks. He quickly packaged them and sent them off to a number of individuals in various levels of law enforcement and government. He gave them all that he could find and access, all save the events that had occurred the previous night. Of last night's events he took a different route, destroying all evidence that had occurred from the company's systems, eliminating all copies of the recording, wiping all memorandums associated with the program, and deleting all files associated with CRISPER11.

After the virtual packets had all been sent and the other files deleted, he created a single physical copy, which he packaged in a small unassuming box. He then wrapped the box in a simple, bland brown packaging paper. On his way to the office he took a detour to a quiet part of the city and handed off the box to a personal carrier, a holdover from a bygone era when people interacted with each other. The courier accepted the package and the payment for delivery and quickly set off to deliver the box, unaware of the magnitude of the package and the implications that it would bring.

The researcher's next stop was the company's main campus where his office was located. Arriving at his research floor he quickly moved to his office where he immediately engaged the privacy screens shutting himself off from his research team. His team exchanged nervous glances, never before, as far as any could recollect, had he arrived late to work. No one dared approach his office, hoping to quickly complete his or her tasks and disappear for the day.

Time passed slowly and quietly, nothing heard beyond the hum of the computers and the click of the keyboards. Shortly before noon the relative quiet was shattered by the sharp crack of a firearm being discharged. The sound originated in the researcher's office and the red stain on the suddenly transparent windows stood as a witness to what had occurred. A single message was carved into the office's table, saying, "You cannot own the soul of the individual."

17

As the sun raised its fiery head in a resplendent dawn it burned down upon the two travelers. Cradled in the arms of the nameless one the girl slept, quietly, peacefully as he carried her along into an uncertain future. It was the first time that she had slept since the incident so many years ago. The nameless one walked on, shielding her from the rising sun and its burning rays.

18

The courier approached the residence in question and knocked. There was no intercom on the building and his directions did not allow him to leave the package on the doorstep. After a few minutes of waiting, he knocked again, this time louder and with more force. When there was still no response, he chose to kick the base of the door, instead of hurting his hand.

After thirty seconds of kicking the door he heard a voice from inside yell "alright, I'm coming! Quit trying to break my door."

Halting his kicking and taking a step back, the courier waited for the door to be opened. When it was he immediately forced the delivery registration form into the man's hand, requesting a signature before handing the package over. The courier was in a rush to complete this delivery and get on with the next one. Once the signature was received, the package was handed over, and the courier was off leaving the man holding the package with a quizzical look on his face.

The man, a former officer of the law, was a private investigator specializing in recovery operations. As the investigator reentered his residence he locked the door behind him before walking back to his study with the package. Once in his study, he locked the study's door and then opened the package and spilled its contents upon his desk. The top researcher's single physical copy of the all that had occurred cascaded into a small mess upon his desk. Randomly picking up a portion the investigator began to read, compelled by an innate curiosity. As he read his eyes grew wide as recognition dawned.

Hurriedly he rushed to the far corner of the room and pulled back a false portion of one of his bookcases to reveal a safe. His hands shaking with anticipation it took him three tries to get the combination right and to be able to open the safe. Inside lay a single leather bound notebook, worn with age and use. Carefully he pulled the book out, opened it, and began to read from it as he made his way back to his desk. It was his last remaining item from his time in law enforcement, and the reason for the end of his otherwise spotless career.

He spent the remainder of the day going over and comparing everything in the book with the evidence provided by the as yet unknown source of the package.

When nightfall came he was ready. He left his residence and quickly made his way towards the area of the city occupied by the rich and powerful members of society. Though he was no longer a member of the law enforcement community, he had a duty to perform, an oath to protect society that he still had to fulfill.

19

A rapidly self-replicating and distributing message began to quickly make its way around the world. The message contained a single video file, the last recording of the company's top researcher. He outlined the burdens of his life, his eternal torment, his life of subjugation, and his apology for what he had done. His message ended with the same message he had carved into the office's table, being "You cannot own the soul of the individual."

20

The government's response was swift and powerful. It was the largest mobilization of force for a single operation resulting in the seizure of company facilities all across the nation. Foreign governments conducted their own raids with varying degrees of success. Personnel were quickly arrested and property seized, some making its way into evidence files, while others were diverted to black sites never to see the light of day. A few private vultures and corporations were able to secret away their own shares of the stash, as fodder for their own research programs.

The company's headquarters campus was the last to be taken, with security personnel valiantly standing guard and refusing access in the face of overwhelming government force. In the end they would surrender, but not before holding out for three days.

In the end, the company's downfall and its top researcher's final message spelled the end for the pink market. Overnight its value collapsed and government intervention would invalidate current investments, freeing millions from the burdens of the market.

21

She looked up from her desk, unfazed by his entrance. The setting sun framed by the window behind her, its fiery hues burning the glass façade of the company a brilliant orange. She waited for him to break the silence, allowing the quiet to calm her fears. Her stoic face gave no indication of the raging fear inside of her.

He spoke quietly, as one who had journeyed far and seen much, saying only, "it is time."

"I knew it would be you," was her only response.

And with that statement it ended, the salesman collecting another final payment for the book of life.

Born in Western Pennsylvania, Logan has spent much of his adult life traveling and living throughout the United States. He currently resides in Western Pennsylvania with his wife and two children. He is an alumni of American Military University, where he completed a Masters of Art degree in Intelligence Studies.

www.ingramcontent.com/pod-product-compliance
Lightning Source LLC
Chambersburg PA
CBHW032043180726
48284CB00008B/2731